THE CRAZY ADVENTURES OF PAUL

A Romance Book about Family, Friendship, Sex and Betrayal.

Margaret J. Herren

COPYRIGHT

All rights reserved. No part of this publication may be reproduced, distributed, or transmitted in any form or by any means, including photocopying, recording, or other electronic or mechanical methods, without the prior written permission of the publisher, except in the case of brief quotations embodied in critical reviews and certain other noncommercial uses permitted by copyright law.

Copyright © (Margaret J. Herren), (2023).

TABLE OF CONTENT

Chapter One

“That stupid bitch!” Paul cursed under his breath as he slammed down the phone. If the second quarter numbers weren’t so good, he might have been in a truly terrible mood by now, but luckily Micheal was just updating him on the booming South African market when the phone rang. “I’m sorry, Micheal,” Paul muttered as he regained some of his composure, “Messy divorce, you understand.” Normally he wouldn’t get so worked up in front of one of his employees, but the drama with his soon-to-be ex-wife seemed to be never-ending. First, she insisted that she get the house and Paul move to a hotel, and now from this most recent phone call with her bulldog lawyer, it seemed like she was trying to take him to the cleaners as far as divorce settlement was concerned. “That’s quite alright, sir, my brother just went through one of those… nasty businesses.” Micheal smiled sympathetically. Paul got the feeling that he could have taken a shit on his desk, and Micheal

would still smile sympathetically: the guy was a sycophant.

“Esther, can you bring in some ice please?” Paul asked his secretary over the intercom. “Yes, sir, Mr. Paul. Right away.” “You feel like a drink before we continue with the South Africa numbers, Micheal? After that phone call, I sure could use one…” Micheal’s face fell slightly, he was eager to continue his presentation, but he wanted his boss’ approval more. “Sure,” he said, “I’ll have a small one.”

Right on cue, Esther, Paul’s assistant, entered with the full ice bucket. She walked over to where Paul was standing at the bar cart and set the ice down on the tray. Paul could smell her soap and her sweet perfume, and just the scent made him hard, reminding him of all the “private dictation sessions” he had with his nubile young assistant. He thought about that first time he ate her shaved pussy and then turned her over and fucked her little upturned ass right on his desk. “Anything else I can get you?” Esther asked

sweetly. She tucked her hair behind her ear and shifted her weight from one high-heeled foot to the other. It was a pity that his affair with Esther (among others) had cost him his marriage, but damn, he thought, as he coveted her tight little body in that hip-hugging skirt, it was probably worth it. “No thanks, darling’,” Paul smiled at her, “I’ll call you if I’ve forgotten something.” He followed her jiggling ass as she sauntered to the door and shut it behind her. Paul poured two double whiskeys on the rocks and handed one to his colleague.

“Here, Micheal, that’ll put some hair on your chest,” Paul said as he handed him his drink. He quickly downed his own and grimaced. “I’m telling you, this living out of a hotel is getting boring.” Micheal was enjoying his boss’ sudden casual demeanor. He normally didn’t confide in him about any personal matters, and Micheal wanted to take advantage of the situation. If he didn’t get that promotion soon, he’d never hear the end of it from his wife. “Paul, how would you like to come over tonight for a home-cooked

meal? My wife, Laura, is making her signature rice. Might be better than room service… what do you say?" Micheal asked hopefully. He could see himself whooping it up with his boss over a wholesome meal, his wife and his daughter smiling and laughing, and then Paul offering him the vacant general manager position… "No, I couldn't trouble you," Paul replied. "It's no trouble at all. Laura's been begging me to ask you over for months. You will be our guest of honor: I insist you come over for dinner." Paul thought for a minute. It was clear Micheal was trying to win the kiss-up sweepstakes here, that this was some kind of tactical move to ask for a promotion. But, a home-cooked meal sounded amazing, and after the month he's had, it might be just what he needed. He nodded and smiled, "Sure, I would be honored." "Wonderful! I'll make sure Esther gets the address, and you can come by at seven. Laura will be thrilled." Micheal couldn't believe his luck. After meeting his charming wife and daughter and eating one of Laura's delicious meals, the promotion would be as good as his.

The rest of the meeting went well, and by the time Micheal left his office, Paul was in better spirits. He thought he might call a little meeting with Esther to celebrate. Now that his wife had left him, Paul was more insatiable than ever. "Hey, Esther? Can you come in here, please?" Paul asked over the intercom. Esther giggled to herself and grabbed her notebook, even though she knew she wouldn't need it. Her boss always had a certain tone to his voice when he wanted more than just a memo taken care of. She didn't mind she loved the attention from her handsome boss, and she knew the ongoing divorce proceedings had to be stressful for him. "You called, sir?" Esther said and closed the door behind her. While she never dressed inappropriately, Esther's curvy hourglass body could make even the frumpiest of businesswear seem provocative. The tight black pencil skirts she wore, accented by high heels, always seemed to hug her round butt, and the red blouse she was wearing today was cut just low enough to expose

a hint of her mouth-watering breasts, her fat nipples poking through the silky material.

Paul smiled at his sexy young assistant. He pushed away from his desk and leaned back in his chair. Esther smiled, dropped her notebook, and kicked off her high heels, sauntering towards her boss with a provocative little wiggle in her step, and then knelt between his legs. She reached for his belt buckle with her manicured hands and undid his trousers. She ran her fingernails lightly over the growing bulge in his boxers and looked up at him, licking her lips. She reached into his underwear and pulled out her boss' massive cock, which was not even fully erect. Paul leaned back in his chair and dreamily closed his eyes as his 24-year-old assistant wrapped her red pouty lips around the head of his cock and sucked him into her warm, wet mouth. Esther had never had such a big cock before she met Paul, but as soon as she had him in all three of her holes, she was addicted. She sucked and slurped happily on his monster cock as it grew and stiffened to its full size. She

wrapped her fist around the base and still had more cock to spare, which she tried to take as deep down her throat as she could. Paul watched his pretty young assistant service his cock and sighed contentedly. He loved watching his big dick slide in and out of her mouth, her thick lips straining to stretch around the plum-sized head as she drooled and slobbered on his massive meat. She pulled his cock from her mouth with an audible pop, and a long string of wet saliva stretched from her lipstick-coated lips to the head of his swollen cock, which was leaking precum. She wanking his slippery cock with one hand, totally saturated with her spit, and lowered her head and began slathering his heavy balls with saliva.

She sucked each one in her mouth and suckled on it. She moaned as she teabagged his sperm-laden nutsack, and Paul could feel the vibrations through his whole crotch. After a few minutes of this, he was ready to cum. “Open wide,” he said as he stood and aimed his cock at her pretty mouth while jerking his cock roughly.

She leaned back and looked up at him, opening her red lips wide and sticking out her tongue in anticipation. Paul gave his massive cock a few final tugs and then groaned as the first volley of cum shot out of his churning balls and landed on her waiting tongue. Not only did Paul have a particularly big dick, but he shot huge loads as well, and today was no exception. Thick ropes of milky cum spurted out of his dick and filled her open mouth. He let a few spurts streak across her cheek and nose for good measure. When he finally milked the last drop of cum from his spent cock into Esther's brimming mouth, she swallowed the whole creamy load down, licking the cum from her red lips. "Thank you, darling," he said as he stuffed his lipstick-streaked cock back into his trouser and helped her up from her knees, "you were a great help, as always." He winked at her as she grabbed her notebook and heels. "Oh, and Esther, honey, could you pick up a nice bottle of red wine and some flowers for Micheal's wife?"

****

At seven pm sharp, Paul drove through Micheal's quiet suburban neighborhood and pulled up in front of a beautiful house. Paul had played some tennis at the gym, showered, shaved, and applied fresh cologne before driving over to dinner, and he felt relaxed and in much higher spirits. He grabbed the nice bottle of Cabernet Sauvignon and the bouquet of purple tulips from the passenger seat and walked up the well-lit stone pathway, and rang the doorbell. After a few moments, a woman in her forties opened the door. Paul was 44, but he could have passed for 34. He kept himself in good shape, and the few grey hairs starting to appear at his temples made him look handsome and distinguished. Between his lean, muscular six-foot frame, his handsome face with deep eyes, and his more than average-sized cock, Paul was incredibly attractive by most standards. And that's exactly what Laura thought when she saw her husband's boss on her front steps. "Oh hello, you must be Paul! I'm Laura, Micheal's wife. We're so thrilled to have you in our home." She

welcomed Paul inside, and he entered the comfortable, pleasant entrance hall. She ushered him into the living room. "These are for you, of course," Paul said with one of his winning smiles as he held out the wine and the flowers. Laura cooed over the gifts and batted her eyelashes at Paul. With her wavy hair and her tailored trousers, she reminded him of one of those housewives who wear expensive pearls just to go to the supermarket. She was pretty attractive for her age, but something about her forced smile repelled him a little. "These are just the prettiest flowers, Paul! You are so considerate!" she gushed. Micheal entered the living room, thrilled his boss was finally here in his house. "Look, honey!" Laura said, turning to her husband, "Paul brought us a bottle of wine! This is going to go great with dinner. Why don't you boys have a seat and I'll bring you some drinks?" Paul smiled at his hostess and settled himself on the brown sofa. He and Micheal sat in awkward silence for a few moments before Laura re-entered with a tray of cocktails. "I saw the recipe for these on YouTube," she said,

beaming, “they’re like a new twist on an old-fashioned.” She handed Paul a drink and watched expectantly as he sipped it. “It’s very nice,” Paul said. It was a little sweet for his taste, but the alcohol felt nice after his long workout. “Our daughter should be joining us, she’ll be home from practice any minute,” Micheal said. “Practice?” Paul asked. He forgot that Micheal had a daughter. How old could she be now, fourteen? Fifteen? “Lilian is a dancer,” Laura said, beaming. “We’re very proud of her: she will be applying to study at Bowen University next year.” She held out a picture of a petite 12-year-old girl in a leotard, pointing her toes and leaping. “This is from ages ago.” “She’s very beautiful, Laura,” Paul said, “I see the apple doesn’t fall far from the tree…” Laura giggled like a schoolgirl and playfully slapped Paul’s arm.

Just then, the door opened, and in walked the most perfect girl that Paul has ever set his sights on cat eyes, long hair pulled into a ponytail, a sweet upturned nose, and delicately curved pink

lips like a work of art. Lilian just turned 19, but at 5’2″ and with a slender body, she looks much younger. Paul couldn’t believe that boring Micheal and his tacky wife could have created this angel standing before him. “Hi Mom, Hi Dad, sorry I’m late, practice ran over,” Lilian said, hanging up her coat and putting down her backpack. She wore the plaid uniform kilt of the local all-girls school, and the short pleated skirt showed off her sleek, smooth legs, stopping inches below her rounded ass. Paul was instantly hard. “Lilian, come meet Mr. Paul, your father’s boss,” Laura said and ushered the pint-sized goddess into the living room. “Nice to meet you, Mr. Paul,” Lilian said and shook Paul’s hand. Paul smiles warmly.

Chapter Two

"Please. Call me Paul," he said. She wrinkled her nose as she smiled at him. Lilian went to help her mother in the kitchen, and Paul studied her as she walked away; her small white shoes, white ankle socks, short plaid kilt, and sky blue polo shirt, the long ponytail hanging down her back that swishes as she walked. Good God, thought Paul, I've never seen anything so perfect. "She's lovely," Paul said to Micheal, still wondering how this short guy with glasses and bald hair could have ever produced such a miraculous offspring. Micheal smiled. "We're very proud of her," he replied. "Alright, boys, dinner is served! Come find a place at the table!" Laura called from the dining room.

Dinner was fine enough, made even finer by the red wine brought by their guest. They told some work stories, and Laura laughed a little too loudly at everything Paul said. A couple of times, Paul looked up from his plate to catch Lilian staring at him with her cat eyes. The first

time he caught her, she smiled and looked away, but after that, he was pleased to find her meeting his gaze, her eyes twinkling mischievously. Lilian couldn't help thinking that Paul was the most handsome man she had ever met. At 19, she's never had a boyfriend, but not for lack of offers. She's had several boys from the neighboring boy's school ask her out, but they just seemed like little boys to her. Some of her girlfriends went out with boys her age, and from their stories, they sounded like total animals. She figured she wasn't missing that much. She always imagined herself with someone older and more experienced, so she resigned herself to waiting until university to start dating. Besides, dancing took up too much of her time to bother with boys anyway.

After dinner, Micheal and Laura were clearing off the plates and cleaning up, and Paul and Lilian wandered into the living room. "So, your mother tells me you're a dancer?" he asked her, desperate to start any conversation with the bewitching girl. "Yup," Lilian grinned, "I was

all-around state dance champion last year." "I bet you're great," Paul said, trying to picture her petite body in those skin-tight leotards. "I'm not bad," she giggled and squirmed her hips from side to side. Paul felt his trousers getting tighter. He settled himself on the arm of the sofa. "Show me some," he said. "Now??" Lilian laughed bashfully and covered her face. "Please?" asked Paul; he smiled a slow warm smile at her. "Okay, fine," she agreed. She stood in the middle of the living room floor and bent one of her slender legs, sliding her right foot up the inside of her thigh. She extended the leg and grabbed onto the sneaker with her right hand, and pulled the leg up to her ear in a full-standing split. Paul could almost see under her short skirt, but not quite. "That's incredible," he said. "Show me another." "Another, eh?" Lilian thought and released her leg back to the floor. "Oh, I know." The petite girl planted her palms on the floor and kicked her feet up to a handstand. Her short plaid skirt fell over her head, revealing a pair of white cotton panties. Slowly, while balancing on her hands, Lilian opened her smooth, creamy legs

wide, stretching into a straddle split. Through the white cotton panties, Paul could see the soft bulge of her pussy, the flimsy material pressed into the cleft of her labia and delicately wedged into the deep groove of her round asscheeks. Paul was overcome with the urge to press his face into the dancer's crotch and inhale, lick her pussy through the damp fabric. "Lilian!" Laura yelled, coming into the living room, "I can see your panties! Come down at once."

The girl came out of the pose gracefully and stood up again. "It's just my leotard, Mom," Lilian shrugged. "It's not decent, not in front of our guest. I'm so sorry, Paul." Laura put down a tray of coffee on the table and went back into the kitchen. "I'm sorry, Mr. Paul, did I offend you?" Lilian asked innocently. The skin between her eyebrows wrinkled in concern. "No, not at all, Lilian, don't be ridiculous. I asked you, remember? I thought you were marvelous." Paul winked at Lilian, and she felt her stomach flutter a little. Suddenly, she felt a little daring. "It wasn't my leotard," she said, a slightly naughty

his cock stir as he tried to picture what she looked like under her panties… does she shave those sweet little pussy lips bald? Paul couldn't wait to get home and jerk off, get that sweet little squirm out of his system. Finally, he stood and yawned and politely took his leave. "Thanks for everything," he said, kissing Laura on both cheeks, much to her delight, "dinner was delicious and your family is lovely." "You're welcome anytime," Laura said, dazzled. She was positive the evening was a success. "See you back in the grind, Micheal," the two men shook hands, and Paul walked outside into the night air. As he walked down the walkway to his car, he looked up and saw Lilian looking down at him from her window. She was wearing a short, ruffled, white nightgown. She smiled and waved to him. She is so delightfully, refreshingly innocent, Paul thought, unlike any of the other women I've been with…

When he was in school, Paul seemed to attract only the experienced girls, and if he was being honest, he never made time for any virgins. They

always seemed like a lot of effort to him, and it never felt worth it. Even his ex-wife had many wild escapades before they met, and he was totally fine with that. But now, something about Lilian's inexperience and simplicity tugged at his heart. He was overwhelmed by his desire for her… Up in her bedroom, Lilian watched Paul wave, then get into his car and drive away. She has felt wet and tingly between her legs since their interaction in the living room. She lay down on her bed and imagined what it would be like to kiss him, and she found herself sliding one of her hands under the elastic waistband of her cotton panties. She parted the wet flesh with her fingers and glided them back and forth over her swollen clitoris. She tried to picture what Paul looked like under all his clothes.

Chapter Three

Lilian stifled a moan as her pussy throbbed and tingled. I have to see him again, she thought.

****

Esther was in for a workout the next day. Paul had called her into his office the second he came in and wasted no formalities as he laid her on his desk and peeled off her black panties. He pushed her legs up and back and started feasting on her shaved pussy and puckered asshole. Esther loved it when he ate her out, and today he licked and sucked at her wet holes as a man possessed. After about ten minutes of licking her out, Paul pulled out his mammoth cock, and slowly fed his pulsating python into her slick cunt. Esther moaned as he filled her full, as she tried to adjust to the sheer size of the massive fuckstick stretching her pussy open. He fucked her hard and fast, and with every thrust, his big heavy balls clanged against her winking asshole like a brass door-knocker. Paul looked down at his

sexy assistant, moaning and writhing beneath him. She was sexy as hell and only four years older than Lilian, but something about her sexiness seemed rehearsed all of a sudden: the red lipstick, the high heels, the black lace panties worn especially for his benefit… He closed his eyes as he fucked away, stretching her tight cunt open with every thrust, trying to imagine Lilian instead: her soft pink lips… but his secretary's throaty whimpering and moaning brought him back to reality.

Paul grabbed Esther's lacy panties off his desk and shoved them in her mouth to muffle her moaning as he felt that familiar tingle building in his balls… The boss had just finished blowing his huge cum inside his squirming secretary when the phone rang. Esther was pressing a couple of tissues up against her overflowing cunt to stem the flow of Paul's semen before she ran to the restroom to clean herself up. When the phone rang, she stood there helplessly, her black panties around her knees. "That's okay, darlin', you clean yourself up," he said to her, "I'll get

this." Esther smiled gratefully at Paul, pulling up her panties and scuttling quickly to the ladies' room before more cum leaked out. Paul reached over and picked up the phone.

"Paul Obikwe," he said. There was a small pause at the other end of the line, and then a small sweet voice said, "…Paul? Hi. It's Lilian Micheal." Even though he had just blown a massive load, Paul's cock stiffened again when he heard the young woman's voice. "Hi, Lilian. How can I help you? Shouldn't you be at school?" he asked, settling into this desk. "Um… I'm sorry. Maybe I shouldn't have called you," the young lady said, "I just… I wanted to see you again." Paul's heart felt like it was pounding in his throat. "Where do you have to be tonight?" he asked in a low voice. "I have practice until 7 and I was going to sleep over at my friend's house. I could always lie and tell my parents that's where I am…" she said, a naughty lilt to her voice. "You bad girl," Paul smiled into the phone. "I'm staying at the Protea Hotel at Ikeja," he said, "Do you know how to get

there?" "Sure, I think so," Lilian said, now she was smiling, "I've taken the bus around the area before. I can probably be there by eight." "Eight it is, then," Paul said, "Room 45." "Okay, gotta go," the teenager whispered and hung up the phone. Paul leaned back in his chair and smiled. He couldn't believe his luck.

****

At eight o'clock that evening, Paul had just settled into the armchair with a glass of wine when there was a small knock on the door. Paul went to answer it. Lilian stood outside his room in her uniform skirt and those white tennis shoes again. It took all of Paul's restraint to not pick her up and throw her on the bed at that instant. He knew he had to take his time. "Come in, Lilian," he said warmly. The goddess wrinkled her nose as she smiled at him, and Paul felt the all-too-familiar tightening in his trousers. She set her backpack down in the front room and then rushed into his suite, staring at the incredible view of the city from his picture window. "Wow

what a view," she exclaimed breathlessly, leaning on the ledge and pushing up onto the tiptoes of her white tennis shoes to get a better view. Paul admired her smooth, sleek legs and felt his heart quicken as he caught a glimpse of her white cotton panties peeking out underneath her uniform skirt. Lilian looked back over her shoulder and beamed a giant smile at Paul, and he fought the unbearable urge to bend over the tiny teen, pull down her panties and take her right then. "You have an amazing hotel room," she said. She turned around and perched on the window ledge, biting her lower lip and smiling shyly up at her Dad's handsome boss. "I was so nervous about calling you, and coming here tonight…" she confessed, "but I couldn't face not seeing you again."

Paul smiled and settled back in the armchair. He loved how honest she was. "What can I do for you, Lilian?" he asked, a slow smile spreading across his handsome face. "I wanted to spend time with you alone," the young woman replied, blushing beautifully. "I think you're the most

handsome man I've ever seen, and you make me feel… tingly all over." Paul felt his cock stirring at her adorable, embarrassing confession. "And you mentioned that you wanted to see my panties again sometime so… here I am." Lilian searched his face for a reaction. She knew she was being very forward, and she wasn't sure if she was making a fool out of herself… "I would like to see much more than that, Lilian," Paul said. All of a sudden, he wondered how experienced she was… she seems so innocent, but it takes a lot of daring to just show up like this… she is a woman of nineteen and a beautiful one at that. Could she still be a virgin? She was certainly smiling like one. "I've never done this before," Lilian confessed, "Tell me what to do." Paul couldn't believe his luck. Not only did this adorable lady find him to be sexy, but he could potentially be her first! Paul had never had a virgin before, and he wanted it to be perfect. "Take off your clothes for me, Lilian," he said, still watching the nervous girl from his armchair. He didn't want to make any sudden

moves that would overwhelm her or scare her away.

Slowly, deliberately, Lilian peeled her shirt over her head and dropped it on the chair, revealing her slender torso and perky breasts only covered by a pink flowered bralette. She knew her breasts were on the small side, and normally she was glad for that fact because smaller boobs were ideal for dancers. But now, for the first time, she wished she had bigger breasts, so she would feel more like a woman and less like a girl in front of this handsome older man. She kicked off her white tennis shoes without untying them. Lilian studied Paul's face as she unzipped the short uniform skirt and slid it down her narrow hips, dropping it to the floor. She stepped out of the skirt and stood there before him in just her pink bra, white cotton panties, and ankle socks. Lilian pulled the hair elastic out of her hair and shook her ponytail free; so that the shining strands fell loosely past her shoulders to the middle of her back. She saw his intake of breath and wondered if Paul liked what he saw.

frame curved slightly in at the waist, and Paul traced the line from her flat tummy down to the elastic waistband of her cotton panties, which hugged her slender hips and did little to conceal the soft bulge of her pussy lips. "Turn for me, Lilian," he said. The graceful dancer did a slow spin for him in her underwear, turning on her smooth, slender legs and pointing her small feet in her white ankle socks. Paul studied her mouth-watering buttocks, the twin cheeks like a perfect peach. The cotton of her panties was riding up between the cleft of the pert rounded ass, and he noticed two small dimples in the smooth skin above the low waistband of her panties.

He was overcome by the urge to palm that cute little ass; to smack the soft, pliant flesh; to suck and lick her fresh asshole and slide his dick between the cheeks of her butt. But first, he was going to make love to her. She turned all the way around and looked at him expectantly. "You are so beautiful," Paul smiled warmly at her, and Lilian melted. He stood and walked toward the

naked girl slowly. At 5'2", her head barely came up to his shoulder. He lifted her chin until her eyes met his gaze, and then slowly, he leaned in and pressed his mouth against her soft lips. He certainly knows what he's doing, Lilian thought. Paul deepened the kiss, brushing his tongue against hers. Lilian moaned and wrapped her arms around his neck. She had never been kissed like this before.

Paul reached down and slid his fingers under the waistband of her underpants, and he felt Lilian brace herself and stiffen in anticipation. “Relax, honey, I’m going to make you feel so good,” he said tenderly, and he slowly peeled the cotton panties down her slim hips, dropping them on the floor. He spread her legs and angled his body between them, giving him the perfect vantage point to feast on her sweet sex. Paul looked down at the most perfect little peach of a pussy he had ever laid eyes on, and he felt his mouth water in anticipation. The tender pouting lips of her small pussy were smooth and bald, with only a light patch of golden hair right above the deep split. Paul used his thumbs to open the swollen labia and saw the wet delicate pink folds that ran from the small pink pearl of her clitoris. Clear liquid seeped from the tiny vaginal opening and dripped down, moistening the crack of her ass and the tight pink rosebud between her cheeks.

Lilian sighed as Paul lowered his head to her crotch and tenderly kissed her creamy inner

thighs, and then planted a kiss on each of her hairless lips. He started lapping at her pussy, gently flicking her clitoris with his tongue, savoring the sweet, tangy taste of her juices. Lilian began moaning, stars bursting behind her eyes in pleasure. She had never had any man make her feel this way before, and she never wanted him to stop eating her pretty pussy. It would have been a challenge even if he had a normal-sized cock, but Paul knew that Lilian would need a lot of preparation if he was ever going to fit his giant cock inside her virgin pussy. As he continued to suck on her tiny pearl, Paul eased his pinkie into the tight entrance of her sex, and Lilian whimpered in response. "Does that hurt you, baby?" Paul asked, watching her face with concern. "No," Lilian responded, "it feels so good…" Paul pulled his littlest finger from her wet hole, licked his index finger, and slid it inside. Lilian panted as she adjusted to the intrusion. Paul gently sawed his digit in and out of her tight pussy and suckled on her clitoris, sending her into orbit.

The tiny teen gasped and bucked against his mouth and finger as her body shook with the powerful orgasm. Paul slid his finger out slowly and looked into her eyes. He brushed the sweaty strands of hair out of her face as she came down, cheeks flushed and gasping for breath. "Wow…" Lilian sighed. She had never felt anything so wonderful. "I want you to fuck me, Paul: take my virginity, make me a woman," she said to him, looking up at his handsome face. "Are you sure?" Paul asked. His heart was pounding in his chest, his cock longing to bust out from the restraints of his trouser. "I've never been so sure of anything in my life," Lilian sighed. "We're gonna have to go slow, honey, I don't want to hurt you," Paul said, pulling his shirt off. Lilian sat up and watched him unbuckle his trousers and slide his trousers and underwear down in one smooth go. Lilian's eyes widened as Paul's thick long erection sprang free. She looked up at, Paul and he could sense the fear in her eyes. "You're so big…" she said, "Will you be able to fit?" "Let's just go one step at a time, okay? I just want to make you feel good, Lilian." Paul

leaned down and kissed her sweet cinnamon-flavored lips. As he kissed her, he eased his finger inside her again and tried to open her up a little in preparation for his thick cock.

Her tight opening was slick with her sweet cum making it easier for his thick digit to slide in and out like a small dick. He pulled the finger out and rubbed it over her tender pink nub while he leaned his face down and drooled some spit onto her pussy. Then he lined up both his index and middle fingers at the opening of her vagina. "Take a deep breath, Lilian," he instructed her. He watched her tiny tits rise as she breathed in. "Now breathe out," he said. As Lilian slowly exhaled, Paul slid his fingers into her tight sheath. Lilian winced. "That hurts a bit," she said, wrinkling her nose in discomfort. "It's so intense…" "Breathe through it, baby, it will go away soon," Paul said, holding his fingers inside her and stroking her taut tummy with the other hand. Lilian panted as she adjusted to the intense stretching of her tiny hole. Paul looked down at

her tender pussy lips wrapped tightly around his intruding fingers.

His cock throbbed, longing to be inside her. After a few moments, he spread his fingers apart slightly, stretching her open more. Lilian groaned. “Bring your knees up to your chest, Lilian,” Paul told her, and the teen raised her pointed feet, bending her slender legs into her chest. Her labia spread open a little, and he could see the pink knot of her asshole appear between her soft buttcheeks. Keeping his fingers inside her, Paul lowered his mouth to the tiny dancer’s butthole and began lapping at the crinkled pink opening. “Ohhhhhh…” she moaned. He was licking her asshole! It felt so good and yet so dirty… Paul felt Lilian’s pussy loosen its vice grip on his fingers, allowing him to see them in and out of the squirming girl’s tight hole while he continued to rim her tasty little ass. Lilian had never been so aroused in her life. Her little clit throbbed as she enjoyed the sensation of her father’s handsome boss lapping at her backdoor, his fingers fucking her virgin pussy.

calmed down, Paul stood and walked over to the nightstand and pulled a big bottle of lubricant out of the drawer. Lilian studied his hard athletic form as he walked, his defined arms and strong shoulders, his tight muscular butt, his glistening six-pack abs, and his long thick erection swinging between his legs below that. He was the most attractive man she had ever laid eyes on, and she felt safe with him. He treated her like a sexy woman and an adult, not like a little kid. She couldn't wait for the moment when he would finally make her a woman.

As Paul came to the end of the bed, Lilian sat up and looked at his swollen manhood. She had only seen one up close once or twice before, but this one was by far the biggest. She studied the thick long shaft, the head glistening with pre-cum, and the heavy furred balls hanging beneath it. She had only been given one blow job before, but she did it more out of curiosity than desire. But now, the desire to take that giant cock into the warm recesses of her mouth overwhelmed her. She looked up at Paul and

cock with lube. Lilian watched him slowly massage his shiny cock, mesmerized.

Chapter Five

"Lie back, Lilian," Paul told her, and she lay back on the bed. Paul pulled her bottom to the edge of the bed and then placed her delicate ankles over his shoulders as he crouched down, bringing his thick dick level with the opening of her tiny pussy. His slippery dick fell onto her tummy with a wet plop, and Paul groaned, noticing that even with his balls nestled against her pussy lips, the head of his meaty dick came all the way up past the girl's belly button. It was going to be a tight fit. "Spread your legs a little, baby," he said, and Lilian brought her knees a little wider for him. He grabbed his horsecock and started rubbing the thick, slippery head up and down between her labia from her clit down to her tiny hole, teasing her sex, trying to make his impending intrusion easier on her. Then, when she felt slick enough, he pushed the fat tip of his dick further between her lips and right up against her wet opening, then pushed some more. Slowly, he began to ease the plum-sized

head inside her, steadily gaining entry until the whole head was wedged inside her vagina.

Lilian sucked in a quick breath. Her eyes rolled up into her head as she panted, feeling his giant cock about to split her poor pussy open. "Are you okay, Lilian?" Paul studied her face, wondering if this would be too much for her. Through gritted teeth, Lilian whispered, "Make me a woman, Paul, do it." "You have to breathe, baby," he said. Lilian took in a shaky breath. When she exhaled, Paul thrust forward, pushing past the tight resistance with his thick charger and tearing through her hymen in one go. Hot tears stung her cheeks, but she had never been so happy. It hurt like hell, but it also felt amazing to finally be a woman, to have her virginity taken by this man, she thought. Paul gritted his teeth and tried to keep from moving too quickly. He wanted Lilian to adjust to the feeling of his big dick inside her. Her newly devirginized pussy felt like a tight throbbing inferno around his cock.

breasts. He loved the feel of her sleek, lithe dancer's body and her tiny breasts, both handfuls topped with a pointy nipple. Paul pushed himself up on his hands and looked down at the angel below him, her eyes glazed over with lust, her knees up by her ears, her tiny feet resting on his muscular shoulders. "Fuck me, Paul," she breathed, "Please fuck me now." Slowly, Paul started sliding his cock in and out of Lilian's tight quim in earnest, her clear lubrication making an easier passage for his pistoning cock. "Ooooh ooooh oooohhhh…" the teenager howled as Paul continued to fuck her tight pussy, his muscular butt flexing rhythmically as he pushed into her rapidly widening hole again and again.

Remembering how amazing it felt to rub herself while being filled full at the same time, Lilian snaked her small hand in between her slender thighs and diddled her swollen clit while Paul's monster cock pistoned in and out. For the third time that night, Lilian bucked and shivered in orgasm, her teeth chattering as her cunny

throbbed and squeezed Paul's swollen cock. "Aaahhhhhhhhh…" she cried and gripped his arms with her small fingers. This pushed Paul over the edge: he pulled his wet cock from her spasming pussy and spurted his thick load all over the squirming girl's tummy. "Unnnngghhh," Paul groaned; it felt like his churning balls turned inside out as he came. White pearly cum pooled in her belly button and dripped onto her tiny bush as he splattered her body with his huge load.

"That was so cool…" Lilian sighed, still light-headed from her powerful orgasm. "Stay right there, honey," Paul told her, and he went into the bathroom, turned on the sink, and rinsed the combination of Lilian's blood and his cum from his dick. He wet one of the washcloths with warm water and brought it out to Lilian who was still spent on the bed, her legs splayed open, her slender mid-section coated in his cum. He bathed her deflowered sex with the wet cloth, cleaning away any residue of their lovemaking from her tender pussy, and then wiped his cum

from her trembling tummy. “Did I bleed on you?” Lilian asked, concerned when she saw the evidence of her broken hymen on the washcloth. “It’s okay, baby,” Paul whispered, “It’s perfectly normal to bleed the first time you become a woman. How do you feel? Does it hurt much?” “I feel amazing,” Lilian said, “it only hurts a little… can we do it again?”

Paul laughed. “Give me a few moments and I’m sure I can arrange that…” he said, smiling. God, where did this perfect little nympho come from? He wondered, thanking his lucky stars. He kissed her cheekbones and the bridge of her upturned nose. Lilian giggled in response. Paul got an idea. He got up, walked back over to his armchair, and sat down. Lilian sat up, watching him curiously. “Come here, Lilian,” he said, beckoning her with his finger. The naked dancer walked over to him gracefully, clasping her arms behind her back nervously. What was he up to? She looked at him expectantly. “I think what I like, while I’m recharging, is a show,” he said, smiling wickedly. “A show?” Lilian asked,

furrowing her brow in confusion. “Yes, I loved the little show you put on for me in your living room last night. I would like to see more of your moves.”

Lilian smiled in recognition. Does he want a show? I can do that, she thought. “Okay,” she said, gauging how much space she had to maneuver, “How’s this?” Lilian raised her arms and then planted them on the carpet, kicking her legs up and over her head gracefully in a cartwheel. As her right leg came back down on the other side of her hands, she slid it forward through her planted hands, landing on the floor in a perfect split. “Tada!” Lilian said triumphantly, raising her arms over her head with a flourish. Paul studied her flexible back as it arched, her slender legs open wide, her hips pressing her little bush into the carpet. She was exquisite. “Another,” he begged. Lilian smiled and pivoted her hips, arranging herself into a perfect straddle split. Paul saw her bare pussy lips spread open as they pressed into the carpet again, and he felt his cock stirring slightly. She

leaned forward on her forearms, pressing her tummy down, arching her back, and raising her ass while pushing her hips through the split, so her legs swung around behind her. Then in one graceful movement, Lilian kicked her legs up over her head and balanced on her forearms. Paul savored the view of her round rump as she straightened one leg behind her and bent the other, pointing her dainty feet.

Paul could feel his breathing tighten a bit as she slowly lowered her pointed feet to the floor in front of her face, one by one. She pushed up onto the palms of her hands; her lithe body arched into a perfect backbend. The creamy skin of her flat tummy was stretched taut as her spine arched up to the ceiling, her delicate ribs showing slightly, and her tiny breasts flattened against her chest. Her hair brushed the carpet. Lilian knew she was giving Paul the perfect view of her exposed pussy as she opened her knees and pressed the balls of her dainty feet into the floor. “Stay just like that,” Paul whispered, and he knelt in front of her spread

legs and studied the bare pussy lips between them. He ran his fingers over the patch of downy hair on top of her pubis, then leaned forward and began licking the dancer's pussy as she balanced in this awkward position. Lilian shivered and sighed as Paul sucked and slurped at her tiny sex. Lilian's lithe dancer's body was such a turn-on to him, and he felt his cock stiffen into what must have been his fourth erection of the day. Paul took each of her calves in his hands and lifted them off the floor, pushing Lilian back into a handstand. "Open your legs for me, like you did last night," he told her, and Lilian obeyed, stretching her straight, slender legs into a perfect straddle split in the air. Her whole crotch was now open to his hungry gaze. The smooth labia separated slightly, revealing the mouthwatering pink flesh inside and her swollen button peeking out from its hood. Paul held the tiny girl upside down, supporting her hips with his strong hands while he buried his face in her sweet bald pussy like a starving man. Lilian's arms shook as she tried to support herself through the teasing pleasure of Paul's tongue.

Just as she thought she was going to pass out, Paul stood and lifted Lilian's body, bringing her upper body up to meet his, and she wrapped her legs around his waist, her wet pussy pressed against his matted pubic hair, his now-erect cock resting between her spread buttcheeks. Paul kissed her lips as he carried her to the chair.

Chapter Six

He placed her gently on the floor in front of him and then sat back in the chair. "Turn around," he told her, and Lilian looked over her shoulder at him as she turned slowly and gave him her back. Paul inhaled sharply, his face level with the tiny dancer's gorgeous ass. Lilian felt his big hands run from her lower back down to the round upturned cheeks of her bottom, and she shivered from pleasure. Paul kneaded and squeezed the soft flesh like two small watermelons, then he leaned forward and kissed one rounded cheek, biting into the skin. Lilian moaned. "God, I love this little ass," Paul groaned, caressing the skin again. He spanked one of her cheeks lightly. It

felt so good, that he slapped it again, harder, making a satisfying smack sound. “Owwwwie…” Lilian whined and touched where he had spanked her. She smirked, looking over her shoulder at him. “Why did you do that?” Paul smiled sheepishly.

“I’m sorry, baby, I got carried away. Come here…” Paul pulled Lilian onto his lap and cuddled her into his muscular arms. “I couldn’t help it, your ass asked me to do it.” Lilian giggled and poked him. He reached down and stroked her sore bottom, rubbing away the sting. “Is that better?” “Mmmmmm hmmm…” Lilian nodded and snuggled into his warm chest. “I haven’t been spanked since I was eight years old! But then, I probably deserved it.” “Were you being bad?” Paul asked. “I’m sure I was being a total brat,” Lilian giggles, “I guess I was misbehaving and talking back to my Mom at Church because all I remember is her marching me outside, bending me over her knee, pulling down my skirts and spanking me right there in the church parking lot.” Lilian shrugged. “It was

so embarrassing." "Why am I suddenly looking forward to the time when you talk back to me?" Paul grinned wickedly, giving her bottom a few lights taps as he pulled her into him and kissed her. "I'm gonna pull you over my lap, and this cute little bottom's gonna be in pain before I'm done." "Is that a promise?" Lilian flirted, running her fingers through his chest hair.

"Don't tempt me, young lady," Paul warned, grabbing her tiny hand, "Not if you want to sit down…" Lilian wiggled away from him. She knew she was playing with fire and that she probably shouldn't provoke him, but she had to admit, after the initial shock, she kind of liked it when Paul smacked her ass… "I like to see you try," Lilian said, sticking her tongue out at him. "That's it," Paul said, standing up, "Get over here." Lilian walked to him gingerly, and he grabbed her arm. "Bend over and touch your toes. Now." Paul whispered in her ear. Slowly, the girl bent over and touched her hands to the ground, bracing herself in anticipation. Paul walked around her and gazed lustily at her

adorable upturned ass, her pussy lips peeking through from behind. He rubbed his hand over her soft cheeks, and then he lifted his hand, raising it above her round butt. He lowered his hand to her bare bottom with a resounding smack! And Lilian bit her lip and winced in pain. Paul studied her wobbly cheek, then he smacked the other cheek hard.

He yanked her up by her arm and pulled her over his knee. Balancing her on his lap, Paul started raining down loud smacks on her upturned ass. Lilian fought back tears as he spanked her naughty bottom again and again. Finally, after a few minutes, when he was satisfied with the sound spanking he had given her, he rubbed her reddened asscheeks, soothing her sore behind. Stroking her bottom turned into running his hands all up and down her prone form, and soon Lilian was whimpering, moving against his hands, greedy for his touch. He grabbed Lilian by the waist and lifted her with ease onto the bed, and directed her to kneel on all fours. He pressed his hand into the small of her back,

forcing her to arch her back and raise her ass, and he whispered, “Stay just like that.”

Paul climbed up on the bed behind her, his aching cock now rock hard in arousal. He lowered his face to her ass and started licking her asshole and pussy from behind. Lilian started purring, savoring the feeling of his tongue tickling her little pussy lips and tight rosebud. Paul grabbed for the lube bottle and started greasing up his swollen cock as he continued to eat Lilian’s squirming ass and pussy. “Oh God, fuck me, Paul…” Lilian begged, “Fuck my pussy…” “Yes, baby,” Paul panted, “here it comes…” He aimed his slippery dick at her tight hole and started rubbing it up and down between her wet lips until the head gained a small entry. Once the head was in, Paul pushed into Lilian’s pussy from behind, the petite dancer grunting from the sheer force of his monster dick splitting her open once again. Paul’s thick cock bottomed out inside her, the fat head butting against her cervix with an inch or two left to spare.

Paul palmed her ass cheeks and began fucking the teen doggy style, enjoying watching his greasy cock slide in and out of Lilian's tight pussy. With every stroke, the girl's swollen nether lips clung to his pistoning shaft. He gripped her hips harder and started pulling her bottom on and off his slippery dick. Lilian could feel the pressure growing inside her clenching pussy and luxuriated in the intense pleasure of being Paul's little fucktoy, no longer a virgin but getting fucked like a whore on her hands and knees. "Uh uh uh," Lilian grunted as he pushed into her again and again. Paul started spanking her little upturned ass as he humped her, making her bubble butt bounce. His heavy balls started swinging, slapping at her clit and sending little ripples of pleasure through her entire lower body. Paul looked down between her bum cheeks as he rode her, at his cock sliding in and out of her creamy little pussy. He took his large hands and spread her cheeks wider so he could see her tiny asshole winking at him as he fucked into his petite princess. He licked his finger and started teasing her little butthole, and this sent

her over the edge. “Gaaaaahhhhhh!” Lilian bucked and came, her tight pussy spasming around his swollen cock. Paul held on tight for the ride, but as he felt the walls of Lilian’s cunt hugging and gripping his cock, he felt his balls boiling over. “Baby, I’m gonna cum,” Paul groaned, and, not wanting to nut in her teenage pussy, he pulled out of her now gaping hole with a slurp. As soon as his cock hit the open air, he shot what felt like a gallon of cum all over the tiny dancer’s upraised ass, bathing her soft cheeks and asshole with his thick cum. “Fuck,” he moaned, appraising his handiwork.

Paul grabbed the washcloth and cleaned his spent baby’s sticky asscrack, wiping the sperm from her soft bottom. As the wet cloth brushed over her asshole, Lilian shivered. Next time that little asshole is mine, he thought. But for now, he felt like the luckiest man alive. Lilian snuggled into his warm chest, and he kissed the top of her head, holding her small body close. He smiled and chuckled to himself as he drifted off to sleep, the little dancer wrapped in his arms…

"Lilian, my dear," he said, "I think I owe your father that promotion…"

Chapter Seven

“Paul? So what is your feeling about reassigning the account?” Paul snapped out of his reverie. He had just been thinking about the last time he ate Lilian’s perfect pussy until she came in a squealing, toe-curling orgasm. He only got to see his 19-year-old princess on the weekends, and it was driving him to distraction. He might as well have not been in this upper-level management meeting.

“Um, I’m sorry… what was that Micheal?” he asked, trying not to sound too sheepish. “Your feelings. About the account. Should we let the Abuja office handle it? You’ve got a lot on your plate…” Micheal tried not to roll his eyes. Paul’s head had been somewhere else this whole meeting. “Fine… that’s fine,” Paul said. Micheal frowned. It’s not like Paul to just pass up an account. “Great, so it’s decided. Let’s table the rest of the account strategy until Monday… It’s too beautiful a day to not be out on the golf course, right? Meeting adjourned.” “You okay,

boss?" Micheal approached Paul and asked him as the rest of the executives left the board room. "Yeah, I'm fine…" Paul said, aware he had a lot of covering up to do. "Just signing all the divorce papers this week. Making me edgy." "I'm sorry, Paul," Micheal felt sorry for the guy; his ex-wife was surely taking him to the cleaners. "Hey, maybe we can play some tennis later? Take your mind off the divorce?" "Sure, that sounds great," Paul smiled, "I'll have Esther reserve us a court later." "Great," Micheal smiled as he watched Paul walk back to his office. "See you later."

Paul passed his twenty-four-year-old secretary and tapped on her desk. "Office" was all he said as he walked past her and through the door to his executive office. Esther hung up the phone, checked her face in the mirror she hid in her desk drawer, grabbed her memo pad (for show), and followed her boss into his office with a shit-eating grin on her face. "Close the door," Paul said, and Esther closed the door and locked it. "I need you to put our Monday Executive

meeting on the calendar," he said, opening his belt buckle and sliding his trousers and underwear down. His long, meaty cock sprang free, almost at full mast. "Sure thing, Mr. Paul," Esther said, approaching him.

Paul sat down in his desk chair, stroking his cock and staring at his nubile, young secretary. Her black hair was tied up in a flirty ponytail. She brushed her hair out of her big eyes and licked her lips, always painted in her signature red lipstick. She knelt between his legs and began taking over for him, tugging on his growing erection and sliding the shaft back and forth as the tip of his cock swelled to its full size. Ever since Paul had started fucking Lilian, his employee's nubile daughter, his hunger for Esther had waned slightly. Thoughts of fucking the pretty dancer consumed all of his thoughts and fantasies, and their many weekend rendezvous had left him quite satisfied... except in one way. While he fucked her pretty pussy until she was sore and could barely walk the next day, he never attempted to fuck her asshole. Paul

was worried that such a depraved act might scare away his innocent young goddess, and he couldn't risk that. But still, thought's of Lilian's perfectly round dancer's ass and the tight pucker between her cheeks drove him to distraction. He craved her sweet asshole. So until he could take her ass, he would settle for the next best thing: Esther's back door.

Paul looked down at the nubile 24-year-old servicing his cock, slurping away happily as he fucked her face with his long thick member, red lipstick smearing along the shaft. Paul reached towards her upraised rump and pulled her skirt up towards him, exposing the skin of her bare ass. "Good girl," he thought with a smile, "coming to work without panties..." Paul sucked his middle finger into his mouth, wetting it, then slowly snaked it into the tight hole between her rounded cheeks. Esther gasped and moaned, sucking his cock harder as his finger sank deep into the liquid heat of his young secretary's tight backdoor. He fingerfucked her butthole for a few minutes with one, then two fingers, opening her

up while she continued to blow him enthusiastically. Finally, he had had enough. He needed to take her ass. "Bend over," he ordered her. Without any further prompting, Esther got up hastily from the floor and bent over his desk, mashing her round breasts into the tabletop and raising her meaty heart-shaped ass in the air.

He felt like a depraved monster, but Paul craved her ass so much he didn't have time to mess with her pussy today. "That's right, and spread your cheeks," he growled low, stroking his thick meat and staring at the delectable sight before him. Esther reached her red manicured fingers behind her and pulled the fat cheeks of her round butt apart, exposing the winking pucker of her asshole. Esther was no stranger to taking his large cock up her ass, and it showed. The puckered ring showed a slight slackening, and the hole gaped slightly into an appealing "o" before he even slid in. Her bare pussy lips peeked out below her inviting asshole, and he began to rub the tip of his cock between her wet, distended labia as he reached into his desk for

the lube bottle. He cracked the lid and dripped a generous amount on his shaft before pressing the opening of the bottle up against her brown eye. He squeezed slightly and let a dollop of the cold lube coat the entrance to her anus. Before it could run down, he grabbed his greased-up tool and pressed the bell end of his throbbing cock against her wet, gaping hole and pushed. "Unnnfff..." Esther grunted as the slippery head pushed past the rubbery ring with a pop. Paul clenched his teeth, sliding his fat log deeper into her welcoming ass. She didn't need too much time to get acclimated to the sensation of his huge cock invading her asshole, and he didn't give it to her.

He spread her cushiony ass cheeks wide with his palms as he began sliding in and out of her slackening passage. Damn, her asshole looked amazing wrapped around his cock, he thought as he continued to bone her from behind. Her hands now free, Esther snaked her fingers between her legs, diddling her clit happily as her boss began to pound her back door in earnest. Paul savored

the obscene sound of his hard thighs slapping against his helpless secretary's upturned butt and watched her writhing on his desk beneath him.

After a few solid minutes of fucking her ass, he pulled his still-swollen cock out of her butt to admire his handiwork. Her asshole gaped open lewdly, and he moaned at the sight. "Look at that fucking hole gape," he said to himself, pushing apart the fat cheeks with his hands. He watched her open asshole wink and flutter until it almost closed up again and then quickly pushed his dick back inside her contracting anus. He teased her like this for a few minutes, pulling out and tapping the head of his wet cock against her open ass a few times, then pushing back in for a few strokes. Each time he pushed his way back in, he forced more air up her butthole until her asshole squelched and farted lewdly around his pistoning cock as he plowed her hard. She was so wet he could feel his nutsack getting drenched with her liquids every time his heavy balls slapped against her puffy lips. Soon he felt that familiar tingle and pulsing building in his nuts.

Paul always came in copious amounts, but it had been at least 12 hours since the last time he came, and he knew he was ready to blow a huge load. And he decided to do it right up his eager secretary's asshole. "I'm cumming, oh God, I'm cumming…" he panted. He clenched his butt and ground his hips into her, his pulsing cock buried deep in her fleshy ass as he spurted thick jets of his hot jizz inside her.

He felt her hungry asshole milking every last drop from him as he drained his balls with a sigh. When he pulled his softening cock from her ass, a torrent of thick cum bubbled and dripped out of her gaping hole and onto his leather desk chair. "Oh yeah, let's see that load, push it out," he whispered to her. Esther grunted and pushed out with her butt muscles, and some more of his cum escaped with a wet fart and splattered on the gooey leather below. "Now lick up that cum like a good girl…" he said, watching her with pleasure as she kneeled in front of the desk chair and licked up his load like a kitten at a saucer of milk. He watched as one

last drop of cum, still clinging to the rim of her abused pooper, slowly dripped from her ass onto the carpeted floor below his desk.

As he watched Esther's slackened hole start to close up again, Paul's unending appetite turned his thoughts to Lilian's sweet pucker of an asshole. God, how he longed to take her ass, to see her tight, lithe body take his whole cock up her tiny back hole. But he was worried she was too small, that he would hurt her, or worse, scare her off. Paul frowned. But hadn't Esther been a novice to anal when he first hired her? Paul was a man who knew how to get what he wanted. He had figured out a way, and even now, a plan was shaping up in his mind: He would buy his little princess a present.

Paul reached out and patted Esther's soft round ass. "That's a good girl…" he sighed. "And if you don't mind, tell anyone who comes by that I'm out for the afternoon. I have to run an errand."

Chapter Eight

Later that night, Paul poured himself a whiskey in his hotel room and drank slowly as he watched the city below his peaceful 13th-floor window. He looked forward to when his new apartment would be ready, and he could christen his brand new sheets with his sweet little dancer. He was snapped out of his reverie by the sound of his phone vibrating with a new text. He reached for his phone and unlocked the home screen.

Done with practice. Yr place in 1 hr? Lilian.

Paul smiled as he typed his reply.

Excellent dear. Don't change your clothes. See you soon.

A few seconds later, her reply popped up:

Lol… Ok, c u soon!

She had signed her text with little hearts and an emoji of a girl blowing a kiss. Paul chuckled to himself. She showed her age. He reached for the little white box on the windowsill, fingering the pink ribbon he had wrapped around it as a present. His cock stiffened in anticipation. "Be patient," he told himself. But still, he couldn't help but smile.

An hour later, he heard a familiar gentle rapping on his door. He went to answer it and was pleased to see Lilian waiting outside. Her hair was tied up in a bun on top of her head, and her cheeks had a smile. Her tight blue leotard flattened her already tiny breasts against her chest, and the shorts she wore over it did nothing to conceal her lean legs or her tight little ass. She smiled at Paul and giggled. "You wanted me sweaty, here I am." He leaned in and kissed her soft lips. They tasted like strawberry lip gloss. She giggled again. "You gonna let me in, silly?" Paul allowed her entry, and he couldn't help slapping her round little ass as she passed him. "Ow!" she said in fake outrage. "That's what

He leaned forward and inhaled her sweet scent through the fabric. Lilian sighed. “You miss this sweet little pussy?” she said naughtily to him. He moaned and licked at her pussy through the fabric. “Of course I did, my dear, it’s all I think about…” he replied. Well, he thought to himself, almost everything. “Take off your leotard, Lilian,” he said, “and lie down on the bed.” Lilian peeled the garment off quickly and threw it in the pile with the rest of her stuff in the corner. Paul watched her, delighted, as she scampered across the room to the bed, her lithe naked body exposed to his hungry gaze. She climbed onto the bed, swaying her tight ass back and forth at him, teasing him. “On your back, Lilian.” Lilian giggled and rolled over. She grabbed her ankles and brought them back towards her head, opening her delectable little crack for him. “Is daddy hungry for his baby’s little pussy?” she asked naughtily. “Oh, you know I am,” Paul replied as he approached the bed, loosening his tie. A few months as his lover had made her naughtier, bolder.

towards her head, exposing her tight butthole to his gaze. He lowered his head and started lapping at her sensitive ass. “Oh God, Paul,” Lilian moaned, “Yes….” When he tried to wiggle his tongue inside her tight little ass, she instinctively flexed her tiny body, moving away from him; the sensation was too intense. Paul growled and pulled her back to his mouth. He continued to tease his tongue against the tight opening. With his right hand, he began to diddle her clit while he ate her ass; soon, she melted into him, opening herself to his wet tongue. “It feels so wrong…” Lilian moaned, smiling despite herself. She felt so lucky to have found this strong, sexy, more experienced man to initiate her into how wonderful sex could feel. If her friends even had half an idea of what she let him do to her, they would be in shock. Just then, Lilian felt her climax washing over her, and she gasped, her wet pussy and ass spasming around Paul’s hungry lips and tongue. He felt her throbbing, then release in satisfaction.

Paul stood, wiping her wetness from his face, and reached for the box on the windowsill. Smiling, he placed it next to her sweaty, panting face. "Lilian, sweetheart, I got this for you." "A present? For me?" She squealed and sat up as she opened the box, sitting cross-legged at the end of the bed. Paul watched her with pleasure as she untied the pink ribbon and opened the lid, lifting out the small metal object. "What is it?" she asked, puzzled. The shiny metal object had a rounded end, shaped like a teardrop; the other end had a sparkly pink jewel. "Is it jewelry?" Paul laughed, "It's a toy, Lilian, a special toy that gives you pleasure. It's called a butt plug." Lilian's eyes widened. "You mean it goes in your…" She blushed. "Yes," Paul said, laughing at her refreshing innocence, "it goes in your butt." "And that is supposed to feel… good?" she asked, dubious about her new gift. "You like it when my tongue is there, don't you?" he asked, already knowing the answer. "Roll over, I'll show you how to use it, dear. That's a good girl."

Lilian slowly passed Paul the metal plug and rolled over onto her belly as she eyed it with suspicion. Paul pulled a small pink bottle of lube from the gift box and applied a little to his finger and the end of the toy. “Get on your hands and knees, please.” Lilian climbed onto her hands and knees, her small upturned ass facing the end of the bed. She gasped as she felt Paul’s wet fingers slowly circling her asshole; she clenched her butt in response. “Now, we don’t need too much lubricant this time, as you’re already pretty wet, but you just lube up the toy and your asshole and then slowly and gently ease it in.”

Paul applied the tip of the cold metal plug against her wet knot and pushed. Lilian gasped. “Try and relax for me,” Paul requested, “Concentrate on opening up your muscles back there.” Lilian took a deep breath in and out. Paul had bought the smallest size they made, but it was still an invasion of her tiny body. “I don’t know if I’m going to like this, Paul…” Lilian said through gritted teeth. “It’s okay, sweetie, just give it a try, and if you don’t like it, you

don't have to use it." Paul had seen her response to his touch, saw how his tongue and fingers on her sweet asshole drove her wild. He knew that she would grow to like it; she just had to give it a fair chance. "Oh fuck oh fuck oh fuck..." Lilian chanted as the plug slowly entered her tight hole and suctioned itself inside. It was fully lodged up her tight ass. The pink gem sparkled between her ass cheeks. "That's a good girl," Paul cooed, "give it a second for your body to adjust to it."

As a dancer, Lilian was used to pushing through uncomfortable sensations, and as she breathed through the wretched discomfort, she felt her full ass relax slightly. "Try moving around a bit," Paul suggested. The odd sensation was still there, like when her mother used to use the rectal thermometer to take her temperature, but something about it felt perversely good. She reached back and felt the plug with her fingers. "I like the pink jewel part," she said, wiggling her hips back and forth. She climbed off the bed and sauntered around, experimenting with the

different sensations. “I want you to wear it home,” Paul said, “and I want you to practice putting it in and out every day until I see you again. Your ass is in training.” Lilian giggled and looked into his dark brown eyes. “In training for what?” “For my cock,” he replied.

Chapter Nine

Micheal was typing upstairs when he saw lights shining out from under his daughter Lilian's door at the top of the darkened landing. He gently tapped on her door so as not to disturb his wife, Laura, who had already headed off to sleep. "Lights off in ten, young lady," Micheal reminded her through the door, "It's getting late." "Okay, Dad," he heard her say through the door, "I just want to finish this last chapter for school tomorrow." Micheal smiled to himself. So many of his colleagues at work complained about their teenage daughters, bemoaning their irresponsible and reckless behavior: staying out at all hours, having promiscuous sex, drinking, doing drugs, failing out of school… But not his Lilian.

He and Laura had only been able to have one child, but Lilian was a joy: responsible, respectful, innocent, straight-laced, a straight-A student with a full ride to university around September. Micheal sighed contentedly and felt

very grateful. He and his wife were either extremely lucky, or they had to be doing something right. He walked down the darkened hallway to the master bedroom and entered quietly so as not to wake his wife. As soon as Lilian heard the door to her parents' room shut, she got out of bed and walked over to the full-length mirror on the wall. She studied her reflection. At five foot two, Lilian had always been petite for her age, and while she had her small frame to thank, in part, for her success as a dancer, she couldn't help but wish she had a more womanly shape. She lifted her nightgown over her head and dropped it in a pile on the carpet, and stared at her own naked body. She turned sideways, studying her tiny breasts in the mirror. After feeding her Mom some story about regulating her periods, she had finally started taking the pill a few weeks ago, and she wondered, was it just her imagination, or were her breasts filling out slightly? She didn't want huge boobs, as that would interfere with her dance, but even at 19 years of age, she barely filled out her A-cup bra. Her tiny nipples

stiffened in the cool air-conditioned air. She lowered her eyes past her flat stomach and down to her pussy. She often covertly studied her teammates' private areas when they were showering in the locker room, and she was always a little self-conscious about the way her puffy lips made a visible pouch in her leotard. But ever since she started seeing her Dad's boss, Paul, her opinion about her pussy had changed. It must not look as weird as she imagined because he loved the way her pussy looked and told her often, calling it her "perfect peach".

Lilian thought about the amazing tongue-lashing he had treated her to earlier that evening, feasting on her little peach until she came all over his face. She smiled as she remembered the gift he had given her: even now, she could feel the metal plug lodged tightly in her virgin ass. She turned around and studied her round ass in the mirror, looking over her shoulder. Her long hair hung down her back to her tiny waist. Standing on her tiptoes, she reached behind her and spread her little taut cheeks apart, and gazed

thought to herself. She held her breath as she opened the search screen and gingerly typed “anal sex”. She was immediately bombarded with hundreds of images and websites. She typed in “teenager anal sex” and pressed enter. She clicked on the first website. Her eyes widened as it loaded.

The website featured pictures and videos of a girl no bigger than Lilian taking a muscular man’s thick hard cock up her ass in a variety of positions. In one picture, she was bent over a sofa as the man stood behind her, his massive tool stretching her tiny tail hole impossibly wide; in another, he lay on his side spooning her, his tattooed arm lifting her leg high to give his cock better access to her ass. She saw a link to a video below and covertly turned off the sound on her computer before pressing play. In the video, the same girl was balanced helplessly on the handsome man’s lap while he held her legs back and fucked into her widening butthole from below. The girl was moaning and biting her lip, and she played with her tiny pussy while he

bounced her on his cock. Then the man effortlessly lifted her off of his massive cock like she was no heavier than a rag doll, and she could see her open asshole gaping wide before he lowered her onto his impaling dick again. The girl licked her lips and smiled as she took this thorough ass-reaming. Lilian felt her pussy start to tingle and get wet as she watched the rest of the video. It seemed perverse and wrong to let a man stick his penis into such a dirty, private hole, but maybe the perverseness of it was what turned her on. A horniness like she had never felt before coursed through her body, and she felt her stretched asshole throbbing around the metal plug.

The girl in the video's body looked a lot like hers, with small tits that barely bounced even while she was taking a hard pounding, a flat stomach, and a round bubble butt. The only difference was that Lilian kept the tuft of hair growing on her pussy mound and the girl in the video had shaved hers completely bald. Well, if that girl can take such a mammoth cock, I can

probably take Paul's, she thought. After all, taking his large cock in her pussy was once intimidating, and now it was easy. Lilian snaked her fingers in between her slick pussy lips and rubbed her little clit while she imagined the man in the video was Paul, and he was fucking her little asshole. Lilian squeezed her eyes tight and bit her lip as she came in a series of intense spasms.

When she came down from her powerful orgasm, Lilian entered "teen butt plug" in the search engine and studied the images that came up. She found a few pictures that looked like selfies: otherwise, normal-looking teen girls posed lewdly in front of mirrors, exposing the butt plug hidden between their cheeks to an imagined audience. A few of the pictures even featured bejeweled ones like hers. Lilian closed her laptop, grabbed her phone, and stood with her back to the mirror. She bent over and looked between her legs at her open ass in the mirror. She clicked a few photos and then stood up to study them. Looking at that jewel lodged

between her cheeks and her puffy pussy lips peeking out below made her hot again. She picked out the clearest photo and texted it to Paul with a little winking face.

Sitting up in his hotel bed, Paul reached for his buzzing phone and smiled at what he saw. Slowly, he reached his hand under the sheets and sought out his already stiffening cock… "…so are you in?"

Lilian snapped out of her reverie and looked up from her bag. Her best friend, Hadiza, was staring down at her with a slightly annoyed, expectant look on her face. "I'm sorry… what?" Lilian asked. Hadiza rolled her eyes at her. She could barely contain her frustration. "Jesus Christ, have you even been listening to one word I've said??" Hadiza snapped. Lilian shrugged delicately and waited for her friend to repeat her question. Hadiza turned her back to Lilian and started vigorously brushing her hair into a ponytail. Lilian could see in the mirror that her best friend's face has concerted with indignation.

"Sorry, I've just been a little distracted..." Lilian offered by way of apology. She knew she had been acting strange since she started to see Paul, and she could sense Hadiza was on to something. Hadiza had been her best friend since primary school and Lilian had never kept a secret this big from her in her life. She just couldn't risk anyone finding out that she was screwing her Dad's boss every weekend. She immediately felt guilty. "No kidding, you've been distracted," Hadiza muttered into the mirror. "I was saying that my parents rented a car for Bayo and me, and I wanted to know if you and Sammy had decided whether or not you wanted in on it or not. The graduation party is only two weeks away, you know."

Lilian did know. She and Hadiza had dreamed about double-dating to the party since they were in junior school. Lilian had her dream dress picked out before her senior year had even started, and she had been the envy of every girl in her class when Sammy, captain of the football team, had asked her out. But ever since she had

given her virginity to Paul, Lilian had to admit to herself: she had lost some interest in the guy. As is, she could only see him on the weekends, and frankly, spending a Friday night anywhere but in Paul's bed felt like a bit of a disappointment to her. "Oh right, sorry," Lilian said, pulling her leotard out of her bag and heading to the bathroom, "I forgot to ask him. I'll let you know as soon as I can." Hadiza sighed as her friend shut the door of the bathroom stall. She peeled her uniform skirt down her hips and tugged her blue polo shirt over her head with irritation. Why was Lilian acting so strange? Wasn't she excited about the graduation party? Hadiza caught a glance of her hot pink push-up bra and matching panties in the mirror and smiled to herself. Her small breasts looked a lot bigger in the bra. Maybe I'll wear this under my dress, she thought to herself.

In the stall, Lilian quickly peeled off her panties and stepped into her team leotard. She didn't dare change in front of her friend today, as she had a little secret: Lilian had been wearing her

butt plug to school all day. She decided to pee, so she didn't arouse any more suspicion. She felt her asshole clench around the plug as she squatted over the toilet and pissed quickly into the bowl. She couldn't help brushing her fingers over the jeweled plug as she wiped herself and stood up. She pulled her arms through the tight sleeves of her leotard, making sure the crotch of her leotard held the plug snugly in place. Lilian felt a tingling in her asshole and pussy… she was being so naughty. Paul would be proud. She flushed the toilet and exited the stall to wash her hands. She caught Hadiza's eyes staring at her in the mirror. "Hey," Hadiza said smiling, "I think I want to buy some new underwear for the party… you wanna go to the mall after practice?"

Chapter Ten

"I think graduation night's the night..." Hadiza whispered excitedly to Lilian. She bent over, pulling her small breasts out of the sparkling push-up bra, and then lifted her hair off her shoulders and pulled it into a twist. She pouted and widened her big eyes as she posed provocatively in the full-length mirror. Lilian was perched on the bench in the small changing room, sitting between two huge piles of lingerie while her friend modeled for her. "...you mean to do it? With Bayo?" Lilian whispered. Hadiza nodded excitedly. Lilian raised her eyebrows at her friend. "You sure? You've only been seeing him for two weeks!" "Oh, don't be such a killjoy," Hadiza reached out and pinched Lilian, teasing her. "He's hot for me, and unlike you, I don't want to go to university and still be a virgin." Hadiza considered herself the experienced one of the two, and up until this point, Hadiza had always been the first one to try things. Little did she know, thought Lilian. "Besides, we've already done everything else..."

Hadiza said, peeling off the bra. Lilian had been a bit jealous of her friend's breasts until she realized that without all that padding, they were no bigger than hers. "What do you mean everything else?" Lilian asked, suspicious. "Oh my God, you're so innocent," Hadiza snorted. "Last night when we were supposed to be doing homework in his room, he went down on me. Oh, and I sucked his dick." Hadiza peeled the pair of tiny hot pink panties down her slim hips and then stood up. "By the way, I shaved my pussy. What do you think?" She put her hands on her waist and cocked her hip to the side, displaying her naked body to her friend. "Wow," said Lilian, not sure how to respond. Hadiza's pubic mound was shaved bald, and Lilian could see her clit and meaty inner labia peeking out from in between her tiny lips.

"Yeah, I heard that guys prefer to eat bald pussies, and I got no complaints from Bayo," Hadiza paraded around the changing room stall nude and checked out her round ass in the mirror. "Hey, pass me that blue thong." Lilian

fished out a blue thong from the underwear pile and tossed it to her friend. Hadiza stepped into the leg holes and pulled up the tiny panties. Her ass cheeks bulged enticingly around the small strip of fabric, and it barely covered her pussy in front. "Oh this is it," Hadiza said, "Lilian you should get one too. I bet Sammy would like it…"

Lilian picked up the light pink version of the same thong and studied it, smiling. She stood up and slid the thong on over her leotard thing "Oh, jeez, Lilian, you're such a bitch," Hadiza teased, slapping Lilian's ass playfully. Under the thong and inside Lilian's leotard, her asshole throbbed around the fat metal plug. Inside her bag, Lilian's phone vibrated with a new text message. It read:

See you tomorrow night; my sweet L. Be wearing your plug. Paul

****

Paul's jaw nearly hit the ground when he saw the thong. Lilian lifted her uniform skirt as she bent over the windowsill, and he saw the thin strip of pink fabric stretched between her taut cheeks, barely covering her bulging pussy lips below. She reached behind and pulled her cheeks open for him, and he could see the edges of the butt plug peeking out from behind the thong. His cock stiffened immediately. Boy, was he pleased? "Where did you learn to do that?" Paul asked her, amused. "I've been studying," Lilian shrugged. She knew she had pleased him with her display. "Yes, you have, my naughty girl," Paul whispered in her ear, pressing his crotch against her sweet backside. "No wonder you get all A's…"

Paul undressed her expertly, leaving her naked except for the tiny panties. He pulled her face-down over his knees and started rubbing her tantalizing ass, kneading the soft, pliant flesh with his big hands. Lilian purred and moaned in response, writhing on his lap. Paul raised his hand and brought it down, slapping her soft

cheek with a loud spank. He gently rubbed away the sting and then slapped the other cheek, enjoying the satisfying feeling of her bouncing butt under his hand. He spanked her upturned ass until she was wriggling her body against him, her belly pressed against his swollen cock. He peeled her panties off with one quick motion and wriggled his fingers inside her cheeks to find the object of his desire. He grasped the little jewel between his fingers and wiggled the plug back and forth. Lilian gasped in pleasure. Just then, Lilian's phone buzzed, and Lilian wiggled free to silence it. "Sorry, Paul, it's just my friend Hadiza won't stop harassing me about the graduation party. One sec." Lilian impatiently typed her response and then turned her phone to silent. "Oh?" Paul said, watching her, amused as ever, "when is the party?" "Next weekend," Lilian said, "I'm kind of dreading it." "Why's that?" Paul asked. "Because my friend Hadiza is acting like an idiot. She is renting a hotel room to have sex with her stupid boyfriend Bayo and she expects me to cover for her. And all I want

to do is… spend the night with you…" Lilian blushed.

She turned to look at Paul. His shirt was open, exposing his muscular chest, and his trousers were around his ankles. He held his swollen cock in his fist. The bottle of lube was open on the table next to him, and his cock was wet and hard. He jerked it slowly as he watched her naked form. "Come here, baby," Paul whispered, "come sit in my lap."

Lilian smiled as she slowly walked over to the armchair where he was sitting. She turned around and then lowered her heart-shaped ass onto his lap. Paul lifted her legs, and she rested her tiny feet on his thighs. Then Lilian grasped the arms of the chair and raised her butt slightly. She patiently squatted over him while Paul disrobed and adjusted below her until he was naked and holding his slippery cock upright. He pressed the spongy head against the groove of her plump pussy lips until he lined it up with her tight hole, then slowly, she lowered her body,

impaling herself on his stiff shaft. Paul groaned at the delicious feeling of her tight pussy squeezing his swollen cock, holding it in its death grip. Her wet soft lips clung to his thick shaft as he humped her tiny body from below, his whole cock enveloped in her warm wetness.

Lilian let the intense sensations wash over her. After a week of wearing the butt plug, she had gotten used to it, but now, with her pussy stuffed full of his massive tool, she was more aware than ever of the metal plug filling her ass. She moaned and groaned, and Paul quickened his pace, bouncing her light body on his cock. He could feel his heavy balls bounce with every thrust. She gripped the arms of the chair tightly for balance as he reached one hand around, parted her chubby pussy lips with his thick fingers, and started massaging her swollen clit. That sent her over the edge. Lilian came hard in a screaming orgasm, her tight pussy closing around his pistoning cock like a vice. Her orgasm triggered his own, and Paul groaned loudly, emptying his throbbing balls into her

wet, spasming pussy. "Such a good little girl," Paul whispered praise into her ear, his voice ragged while he rode out his orgasm, "that's my perfect little princess…" She rested against his muscular chest while they both caught their breath. He brushed her sweaty hair away and kissed her shoulders and neck.

After a few minutes, he lifted her petite body off of his shaft, and a copious amount of thick, warm cum dripped out of her stretched hole and onto his spent cock. Without being asked, Lilian climbed off of his lap and kneeled between his muscled thighs. She lowered her head and started licking their combined juices from his softening tool. She looked up at him, her cat eyes shining, and licked his cum from her smiling lips. Paul groaned in pleasure. He was starting to feel himself getting hard again. He looked down at her again and held her head between his hands, his fingers tangled in her hair as she bobbed up and down contentedly, her lips suckling on the swollen head of his shaft.

Chapter Eleven

Before he knew it, he was ready to explode again. "Goddamn," he groaned in disbelief, "Lilian, baby, I'm gonna cum…" He pulled his thick wet cock from her swollen lips and aimed it at her a-cups. He moaned as his balls spasmed, spurting two or three thick ropes of white cum in between her tiny tits, her sensitive nipples stiffening as he shot his load. When he came down from his second powerful orgasm of the night, he looked down at her shining face and smiled. "I think we should clean you up a little, don't you?" he asked mischievously. Still naked, he led her into the hotel bathroom and turned on the bath. "Get in," he told her, smiling. Lilian hopped into the bathtub, testing the water with her foot and wrinkling her nose in reaction. "It's lukewarm," she protested. "You don't want it to be too hot," he explained, "You'll get scalded." She watched him switch the water to the handheld shower head, and he pointed the stream of water at her sticky chest. He gently

sprayed her tiny breasts, washing the evidence of their love play away from her young breasts.

The water felt cool and refreshing. “Now get on your hands and knees, honey.” Lilian knelt in the shallow water on all fours, her head looking at Paul quizzically. “No, Lilian, turn your butt towards me,” Paul corrected her, amused at her innocence. Lilian laughed as she wiggled around, so her head was facing the faucet. Her ass was tantalizing in the air, offering him a glimpse of her jeweled butt plug, and some of his pearlescent cum still clung to her swollen, well-used pussy. He parted her nether lips with his fingers, studying a thick drop of semen that was slowly dripping out of her hole and onto her perfect little clit. She shivered as he rubbed his cum onto her swollen clit, and then felt the gentle spray of the shower head as he rinsed her off. When she was all clean, Paul turned his attention to her sweet asshole again. He could hear her suck in her breath as he wrapped his fingers around the edge of the plug and pulled gently.

He worked the plug in and out of her tight back door until it finally dislodged. Lilian shivered and groaned as the metal object slid out of her slippery asshole. Paul rinsed off the plug and set it on the edge of the tub, and then turned his attention to the delectable sight in front of him. Her tiny knot of an asshole, which had gaped open slightly when the plug came out, had already fluttered closed and sealed itself up into a (slightly looser, but still pretty tight) knot again. He ran his finger over the little pucker between her cheeks and groaned his pleasure. When he finally got to take that virgin ass, it would feel so amazing, he thought. "Stay just like that, Lilian," he said as he stood and walked out of the bathroom. He grabbed the bottle of lube off of the end table and a box from the drawer and returned quickly. He squirted a small dollop of the thick substance on his finger and began working it in and around her tight backdoor.

After a minute, he was pleased to notice that his index finger gained quick entry into her warm cavity. “Good girl, Lilian,” Paul cooed as he started to “saw” his finger in and out of her tight tailpipe, “You’ve been practicing, it’s very clear.” “You’re pleased with me?” Lilian asked hopefully. “Oh yes, baby girl, I’m very pleased with you,” he replied. He withdrew his finger and applied more lube. Then he pressed two fingers against her small orifice. She grunted as his thick fingers pushed into her asshole. “Are you okay, baby?” he asked. “Yes, Paul, it just feels so… intense…” Lilian gasped again as Paul slowly started sawing his fingers in and out again. Paul had already cum twice, but he could help but get hard again at this incredible sight. The ring of her open ass clung to his lubed-up fingers with every thrust. Damn, he wanted that tight hole. “Are you going to fuck my ass?” Lilian asked. Paul could hear the worry in her voice. She had come so far since last week, but he knew if he wanted her willing, he couldn’t push her that far today. “No, not today, baby girl,” Paul said to her, still fucking his thick

fingers in and out of her slick chute. He felt her relax slightly in relief. "We're just going to practice opening you up. I promise. Now, Lilian, I want you to play with that sweet pussy for me." He watched her as she reached her slim fingers underneath her and began to rub her swollen clit. "That's a girl." As Lilian played with her throbbing pussy Paul could feel her asshole flower open slightly, giving his fingers even more room to maneuver. "Good girl…"

He rested his other hand on her lower back, holding her in place while he slowly began to separate his fingers in her asshole. She moaned at the intense feeling. "Keep going," he urged her, "just breathe through it." Slowly he scissored his fingers open and closed, stretching her tiny hole until he could separate his fingers a full inch apart. He couldn't help himself: he pooled some saliva in his mouth and then spit into the small opening, perversely enjoying this lewd act. He smiled as he imagined how good it would feel to slide his cock up her well-lubed butthole.

Paul snapped out of his reverie when he realized, much to his delight, that his innocent little princess was hunching her tight ass into his hand, fucking herself with his slippery fingers. That little vixen! He thought to himself. She's a fucking natural…

Paul pushed back at her, fucking his fingers in and out of her greased chute as she quickened her pace, diddling her hanging clit at a furious rhythm. Suddenly, he felt her body shudder as she groaned and panted through a toe-curling orgasm. Lilian felt the tingles through her body as her spasming asshole clenched involuntarily around Paul's fingers.

Finally, she collapsed forward in the tub, his fingers dislodging from her wet ass with a slurp. "Oh my God…" she moaned, "That was incredible…" Paul, pleased with his protegée, wiped his fingers on the bath mat and reached for the box at his feet. He opened it and took out a slightly larger plug, this one with a purple

jewel. He quickly squirted some lube onto the plug and spread it around the bulbous head with his fingers. "Hold your cheeks open for me, Lilian," he instructed. He was pleased to notice that she did as she was told automatically, even as she asked him why. "I got you another present," he replied. He slowly but easily slid the bigger plug inside her loosened hole until it was lodged in place. "What's that?" Lilian asked, gasping at the intense sensation in her still-sensitive asshole. "It's a bigger plug," Paul replied. "This will help get you ready for my cock." "When will that be?" she asked with a shiver in her voice. He could sense her fear but also her anticipation. He had her right where he wanted her.

Paul smiled in response. "On your graduation night. When your friend is losing her virginity to some clueless school boy, I'll be taking your virgin ass."

www.ingramcontent.com/pod-product-compliance
Lightning Source LLC
LaVergne TN
LVHW050319160826
845677LV00014B/3481

* 9 7 9 8 3 7 5 5 1 1 4 1 2 *